After a showdown with Chippy who won the Book-of-the-Year Award with *his* idea, Jimmy gets to keep the prize for a year and fifty quid. New boots *and* a computer (if he can learn to use it – Brains O'Mahony says it's banjaxed).

But Mrs O'Leary is on the warpath. Who's been slagging her by writing on the walls? Who's trampling on the flower-beds on Bray sea front? She suspects Mad Victor and she's out to get him.

That is if she can spare the time. She's started a campaign to reclaim the Town Hall from McDonald's. So she rustles a cow and sets off up Main Street …

# Peter Regan

# RIVERSIDE

## v City Slickers

Illustrated by Terry Myler

THE CHILDREN'S PRESS

*For*

*Claire and Megan Regan*

First published 1998 by
The Children's Press
an imprint of Anvil Books
45 Palmerston Road, Dublin 6

4 6 5 3

© Text Peter Regan 1998
© Illustrations The Children's Press

ISBN 1 901737 07 1

All characters are fictional.
Any resemblance to real persons, living or dead,
is purely coincidental.

Typeset by Computertype Limited
Printed by Colour Books Limited

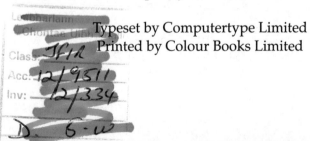

# Contents

# 1 Computer Games

It was no joke propped up against the wall of Lansdowne Road railway station waiting for the the DART to come. It was no joke – with my eyes beady-red from crying. I was all dressed-up: good shirt, good tie, shiny shoes, a brand-new jacket, not to forget my fancy new trousers.

I'd never been as well-dressed in all my life, and all because I'd gone to a daft book-awards 'do' in Jurys, only to find out that my so-called pal, Chippy O'Brien, won the competition with an idea for a story he'd stolen from me. Not just that, but he stuck me with a daft cock-up of an effort called *Forlorn Love*.

I could imagine Chippy back at Jurys Hotel gloating over the computer he'd won for writing the best book in the competition. Already, I was hoping the computer would smash on the ground. I wasn't just hoping – I was praying. Then, just as I was cheering up, I thought of Chippy maybe going into the toilets at Jurys and counting the £100 prize-money that went along with the computer.

There were two men on the platform. They asked me if I was okay. I said I was. But anyone could see I wasn't. I just wished they'd leave me alone, stop staring and that.

But the tears quickly came to an end. Chippy appeared on the platform. He was almost completely hidden by a large cardboard box he was carrying. Only the front of his hands, his head and the bottom of his trousers could be seen. Everything else was a cardboard box. I fought back the tears. I wasn't going to let him see me cry. I did my best to blank my mind and stuffed my sodden tie into my pocket.

He came up the platform towards me.

I turned and looked the other way. More than likely, the computer was in the box.

I knew he'd try to make up with me, over robbing my ideas for the story he'd won the computer and £100 with. I'd have none of it, though. Best pal or not, I felt like hitting him a thump. But the cardboard box was too big to get at him. I wouldn't have the reach. Not unless I grabbed him from behind. I'm not into grabbing people from behind, because that's being sneaky. See, I'm not a sneak. Chippy is though. He's sneaky right through.

'I saw you beltin' outa the hotel,' stuttered Chippy. 'You shoulda waited … I wanted to tell ye about all this … Maybe I shoulda told ye before now … How was I to know ye were goin' to be there …? I was goin' to tell ye when I got home. Know wha' I mean?'

I knew what he meant all right. He thought I was some kind of half-thick, that he could pull the wool over my eyes, no bother. And he had fooled me. There he was with a mountain of a computer and £100 prize-money stuffed in his inside pocket. A computer and £100 I would have won if he hadn't tricked me out of my football story.

Just then, Chippy put the cardboard box down. I took a swipe at him, and missed. Next thing, we were tangled around one another. Only I broke loose and fell across the box.

'There's no need for that. Look, ye've put a dent in the box! You'll banjax the computer. It'll be no use to anyone!'

That gave me an idea. I got up off the box and gave it an almighty kick.

Chippy made a lunge at me. We were in a tangle again. The two men down the platform came up and held us apart.

'What's all this?' they asked.

'Ask him!'

'Ask me? It's nothin' to do with me. It's you. Ye kicked my computer.'

'I didn't. I kicked the cardboard box.'

'Same thing. If it's broken, it's yer fault.'

'It's not my fault.'

'Wha' d'ya mean?'

'It shoulda been mine, anyway. You robbed it on me.'

'I did not.'

Just then, the DART came along. The two men got on. Chippy and me stood glaring at one another.

'Well, are ye goin' to give a hand to carry the computer?' asked Chippy. 'It's part yours.

That's wha' I wanted to talk to ye about, until you jumped on me.'

I felt like telling him to go to hell. But something came over me – the good side of my nature, I guess. So I took hold of one end of the cardboard box, while Chippy took the other, and we got on the DART. Looking back, I know it wasn't the good side of my nature that made me give Chippy a hand; I didn't want to miss the train, that's all.

We sat on opposite seats, with the computer in between. I said nothing, just stared at the dent I'd put in the cardboard box.

Chippy began to chat away like mad, trying to make friends with me. I ignored him. But when he said he'd give me half the £100 prize-money that changed things.

'We'll split the prize money, fifty-fifty,' he said.

'What about the computer?'

'We'll sell it, split the money.'

'Tell you what,' I said, 'I'll have the computer, you keep the hundred quid.'

'The computer's worth at least a thou.'

'Is it?'

'Course it is.'

'I'll owe you the difference then.'

'You will?'

'Course I will.'

And I would, forever.

By the time we got off the train in Bray the computer was mine for a year. Then it would be Chippy's for a year. Then mine, and so on.

What's more, we were friends again – best pals.

And what did I want the computer for? To write another story, of course. Not straight away. Sometime soon, before the year would be out. Before I'd have to hand over the computer to Chippy.

But in the meantime, I had something else in mind. Football! Soccer, the game of the common people.

It was time to get cracking with Riverside Boys.

## 2  A New League

Mr Glynn is our football manager at Riverside Boys. Harry Hennessy is his right-hand man: his assistant. We are all very fond of Harry, only he is more fond of Guinness.

The reason our football club is called Riverside is because our football pitch is beside a river, the river Dargle in Bray.

The Dargle isn't a huge river, but it's big enough. After heavy rain the water drains off the mountains into the Dargle and the swell sometimes gets trapped by the tide coming in from the sea. Sometimes when that happens, there's nowhere for the water to go, except burst the river-bank and flood the streets around our football pitch.

The river isn't supposed to flood any more, because some years ago a big job was carried out to stop the flooding. But it will happen again. It's bound to flood sometime. When it does, Mr Glynn will be one of the first into the boats as his house is just down the road from the Dargle, right in the middle of a hollow. The rest of us won't get flooded though, as most of us live in either Fassaroe or Palermo, and they're up on a height.

If you like Venice, but haven't time to visit, buy a house beside our football pitch; you won't be disappointed.

There are lots of other teams in our football club. They range from U-8 to U-18. (I met someone the other day who didn't know what 'U' stood for – 'Under', that's what it stands for.) Most of the teams are loony, but we're the looniest. I think we're the looniest team ever to play for Riverside Boys. We're not really wanted in any league, but Mr Glynn is very good at persuading people, and he always manages to get us in. We owe Mr Glynn a lot, because only for him we wouldn't be allowed play football. No other club would have us, that's except for Chippy. Chippy is a brilliant footballer. He's that good every schoolboy team in Ireland would like to have him. Chippy's a messer though, just like the rest of us. What's more, he's crafty. He's always on the make, cuter than a fox. Once he sold Harry Hennessy a pyjamas-top and convinced him it was a fancy American-style shirt. Harry wore the pyjamas-top a few Sundays, but had to give up on it once the slagging started.

Mr Glynn doesn't manage all the teams in our club, because there are too many. But he's the main man in the club, and we're proud of him. We're proud of Harry Hennessy too, but for different reasons. Harry is a hero of ours, but I'm not going to explain why because it would only cause trouble. Some things are better not said. But if Harry Hennessy were to die tomorrow he'd have the biggest funeral ever seen in Bray. There'd be so many Harry and his coffin would be lost in the crowd.

Apart from being beside the Dargle river, our pitch is only about a mile from the border with County Dublin. Sometimes we like to think we are a Dublin club, but we're not; we're Wicklow. We have this thing about playing in Dublin – we think it's great.

'We should be playin' in Dublin.'

'Naw, we should be in Wicklow.'

'Why, Chippy?'

'Because we're from Wicklow.'

'Nigger Doyle's not. He lives across the fields from Old Conna Avenue, an' that's in County Dublin.'

Nigger Doyle's our inside-right. Across from Fassaroe there are fields, and across the road from there is County Dublin. Nigger lives in a house beside one of the fields. Most times, if you get up early in the morning, rabbits can be seen in the fields. They have little white buttons for tails, and run like hell if you chase after them. Mad Victor thinks they are hares because they can run faster than him. By the way, Mad Victor also plays for Riverside. He plays everywhere and anywhere.

'They're not hares, they're rabbits, Victor.'

'They're hares.'

'They're rabbits. Hares run much faster, and they don't have those stumpy white tails.'

'There's foxes in them fields too.'

'There are?'

'I saw one once. Then I saw another. I saw two fields full of them.'

'Ye didn't.'

'I did!'

We didn't believe Mad Victor. We knew he could exaggerate. That is part of the reason he is mad.

A few days later we found out which League we'd be playing in for the season. When we went down to the Park for training Mr Glynn and Harry Hennessy filled us in on what was going on.

'You're playing in the Dublin Schoolboys.'

'Wha' about Wicklow?'

'Forget about Wicklow, you're in Dublin.'

'You sure, Mr Glynn?'

'Course I'm sure.'

'Mr Glynn, we were in Dublin before. They threw us out.'

'They didn't throw us out. There was a mix-up. We all thought there was no League in Wicklow, and then there was. That's what happened. We weren't thrown out. A League started up in Wicklow. We had to come back and play in it.'

'Same thing could happen again, Mr Glynn.'

'No, it's all been sorted out. It could never happen again.'

I looked at Chippy. Chippy looked at me. We all looked at one another. No, the same thing could happen again. But we didn't care. All we wanted to do was to play football for Riverside, and have a good time. Once we were in a League, any League, we were happy enough.

By the time training was over we were all

keyed-up to knock the lard out of whoever we'd be playing in the League.

The oul' lads who ran the League were a bit slow, so that meant we wouldn't know for another week the section we'd be in. Meaning, we wouldn't know for another week who we'd be playing against. But, when the time would come we'd be good and ready.

'That so, Victor?'

'Yeah, that's so.'

And so it was.

We were good and ready.

# 3 Banjaxed!

First thing I did when I brought home the computer was to put it on the kitchen table for my two sisters, Fiona and Kathleen, to see.

My da had a good look from a distance.

'Can it work out the results of horse-races?'

'Don't be stupid, Da. No, it can't'

'Then it's no good to me.'

Da is big into horse-racing. He spends most of his time in the bookies. I kept a firm grip on the fifty quid prize-money in the bottom of my pocket. If Da had of known he'd have turned me upside down to get at it. I'd no intention of telling Ma, or my sisters, just in case they'd let it slip to Da. Then I'd be in real trouble. He'd have me plagued for a few bob. Soon as I got the chance I'd go up the town with the fifty quid and buy a new pair of football boots. Maybe, have a feed of chips and vinegar with what was left over. Maybe, bring Mad Victor on a day and night out to the pictures.

When my family finished eyeing the computer I brought it upstairs to the box-room where I do all my writing. I wouldn't be doing any writing for a while, only a few simple poems about my da and sisters. Learning how to use the computer was more on my mind.

I checked the instruction book and set up the computer hardware. Then I plugged it into a socket. I expected the screen to light up and show lots of things to do. Maybe the little arrow that's in computers would move around, show a bit of life. But the screen was dead. There was nothing, just the same blank screen as when I took the computer out of the cardboard box.

I checked the plug to make sure it was properly wired. Nothing wrong there. I checked all the connection points on the computer hardware. There was nothing wrong at all, as far as I could see. I tried reading the instruction manual again. Except for a few sentences, I couldn't make head or tail out of it. There was no use asking my da or sisters, they'd be too thick. As for Ma, she had no confidence. How could you expect her to? After twenty years married to Da, how could she? Da should have married a racehorse; that way everyone would have been happy, Ma included.

There was only one thing to do, I'd have to ask Brains O'Mahony around to the house. He'd fix the computer. There's nothing Brains can't fix, my da's brain excluded. And know why not? Cause Da hasn't got a brain, that's why!

Maybe I told you before, but I don't like my da. I don't hate him either. But one thing, I don't like him. How could I when he loses everything (money) in the bookies!

Brains came around.

'That computer's banjaxed.'

And so it was. It must have been from the kicking I gave it on the platform at Lansdowne Road.

'What'll I do?'

'Bring it back to the makers. Tell them it never worked. It was like that when you got it.'

'Hey, it was made in America. How am I supposed to get it to America?'

'Don't be daft. They'd have agents here in Ireland. There must be an Irish address somewhere.'

'Here's one.'

'Where?'

'Swords, County Dublin.'

'Well, bring it to Swords.'

'How?'

'On a bus. By helicopter for all I care.'

I didn't bother asking Brains any more. He

had begun to give me dirty looks. Probably thought I was as dopey as my da. I brought him down to the kitchen, gave him a cup of tea and a few squashed Mikado biscuits.

'You get that computer out to Swords soon as you can.'

'I will.'

'Don't sit on it. And get a letter from that crowd you won the computer from. Maybe they'll be able to give you a receipt. Whatever you do, get movin' on it straight away.'

'I will.'

And I would.

I would.

# 4 Mr Glynn's Surprise

The week before we were to play our first game in the Dublin Schoolboys League Mr Glynn had a surprise for us.

'Come out to the road, I want to show you something.'

We all trotted out to the road in our mixed assortment of training gear: Riverside gear, Liverpool gear, anybody's gear we'd found along the way.

'What do you think of it?'

He was showing us a Volkswagon minibus.

'Good, isn't it?'

As far as we were concerned any kind of van was good, once it had an engine, and once the windows opened so we could shout abuse at people passing by.

'I got it for taking the teams to matches. We won't have to hire one any more. It'll help save money. And we can use it for other things.'

'Other things' sounded great to us. There

were plenty of other things we could do with the van – go for trips, act the fool, maybe even learn how to drive.

'Can we have a spin in it now, Mr Glynn?'

'No, you've training to do first.'

'After trainin', then?'

'Maybe.'

We eyed the van carefully. The body looked all right, and the wheels. The doors all opened and closed – the windows too. The seats were nice – no rips.

'Can we get in, Mr. Glynn?'

'Just for a minute.'

We piled in, all fourteen of us. There was barely enough room. Three of us had to go across the back. Then there were two double-ups on laps, so as to make sure there would be enough room in the front for Mr Glynn to do the driving, and for Harry Hennessy to sit beside him.

'Mr Glynn, could we not leave Harry at home for away matches?'

'Of course not. He has to come, he's part of the set-up.'

Trust Chippy, asking to leave Harry out. Harry went everywhere with the team. We couldn't leave him out, not even if it meant having to squash together to make enough room for him. A few years ago it wouldn't have mattered. But we were U-15 now, beginning to use up space rapid. Some of us were big lads, nearly six-footers. Sonny Clarke even had a moustache. And all our voices had gone real deep, so deep if they had been water we would have drowned.

The van even had a radio and a tape-deck. We fell in love with it straight away. We fell in love with it that much we didn't want to go back into the Park to do our training. But Mr Glynn made us. Harry Hennessy got up on a bike he'd just bought in some junk-yard and lashed us around the Park ten times. And that was only the warm-up. By the time training was over we were that tired we couldn't untie our boot-laces. And to make matters worse, Mr Glynn wouldn't give us a lift home in the minibus. The only thing that saved us was Flintstone. He is always able for training –

even the toughest lapping and sprinting. He was almost fresh as a daisy, so we loaded up all our gear on him and he carried everything home for us. Flintstone is great; you can use him for anything – even as a camel.

In case you never heard of Flintstone before, he is my mate, just like Chippy and Mad Victor.

Before we went home Mr Glynn told us who we'd be playing against in the Dublin Schoolboys League. We were in the 'B' section. We had never played against any of the teams before, so that meant we'd be going to new places, places we'd never seen in our lives. That made us all the more excited and keen to get on with the new season. It made us feel like explorers, going to all these new places and playing against faces we'd never seen before.

Mad Victor said it made him feel like he was Doctor Livingstone that time he went to explore Africa. But we all knew it wouldn't be as exciting as it was for Doctor Livingstone. We were only going to places like Ballymun, Ballyfermot and the Phoenix Park, and although there would probably be a few black faces there wouldn't be enough to make it as exciting as it was for Doctor Livingstone.

Although Mr Glynn told us who we'd be playing in the Dublin Schoolboys League, I'm going to give some of the teams made-up (by me) names. Brains O'Mahony said if I didn't do that I could be sued. But that wouldn't worry me, because apart from the fifty quid book prize-money, I'm stony broke. Ma and Da are next to broke too. They only have 'here today, gone tomorrow' kind of money. As for the house, it's not ours; it's a council house. We own nothing, except for some furniture and the clothes we wear. One advantage about being broke; it cuts out all the worries rich people have.

Anyway, I'm going to give some of the teams made-up names; the players and managers too. Teams I don't like I'll give daft names to. That way nobody will know who I'm talking about and I won't get into trouble, because football teams are always going to court. Some teams are that bad at playing football the only place they can win is in a courthouse. There is more to soccer than just playing football; there is more to a courthouse than law. Sounds good, doesn't it? It sounds that good I'm going to write it down in a jotter and use it in a story some day.

We could hardly wait for Sunday to come. Mad Victor was like a bull-terrier on a leash, he was that eager. Flintstone was in orbit running around the estate non-stop. Chippy was cool as a cucumber. Me, I had my new football boots soaking in a basin of water.

Most of the others were doing extra press-ups every morning after they got out of bed. We were all fired-up and ready to go.

Us against the world.

Us against Bees' Knees United.

Bees' Knees United weren't exactly a million miles from Bray; they weren't even ten miles from Bray.

They hated us.

We hated them.

Bees' Knees United v Riverside.

There would have to be a winner.

There would have to be a loser.

Hopefully, the winner would be us.

# 5 The Boyfriends

I spent most of the fifty quid on a pair of football boots but I got new shin-guards as well, plus a feed of chips for Mad Victor. That made me broke again, but not quite. You see, Chippy, Flintstone and me have a vegetable round. We sell five barrow-loads of vegetables around the estates every Friday night and most of Saturday. Luckily the vegetable round doesn't interfere with our football matches as we play on a Sunday now. What's more, I have a joint account with Chippy in the post-office. We put most of the money we make from the vegetable round in it. I have fierce trouble with the da, though. Now and again I have to give him money so as he can go out and lose it on the horses.

My sisters, Fiona and Kathleen, don't like the idea of us selling fruit 'n' veg.

'I don't know what you don't like.'

'The whole thing.'

'What d'you mean?'

'The barrow, for one thing.'

'There's nothin' wrong with the barrow.'

'That's wha' you lot think. Yous look like tramps shovin' that thing around the estates.'

'That's because we're doin' well, an' you're jealous. It's because we're makin' good money an' you're not!'

And that was telling the truth. Neither of my sisters have a job, not lately. Once they had no boyfriends either. But all that changed. Ever since my ex-flame, Heather McFadden, made them half-beautiful my da was a nervous wreck trying to keep the fellows away. That was until one day two lads drove up in a fancy car. They pulled in right outside our door. They opened our gate and knocked on our door.

My da opened the door like a light. 'Come in, an' have a cup of tea, lads.'

'We just want to see Fiona and Kathleen.'

'They can wait, 'said Da. 'Have a cup of tea.'

'And a biscuit,' I added, just trying to be friendly.

'Mr Quinn, we just called for a second. Are Fiona and Kathleen in? We'd like to see them.'

'What for, lads?'

'We'd like to take them out.'

I thought Da would have a fit. He was always dead against anyone taking my sisters out. But the two lads' posh accents, and the fancy car outside quickly changed all that.

'Well, ye'd better ask them.'

'We did. They told us to see you.'

Next thing, Fiona and Kathleen came downstairs. They were dressed to kill. They must have spent hours doing up their faces. All of a sudden they'd got sun-tans.

I was full certain Da wouldn't let them out. But he did. He fairly shoved them through the door and walked all the way to the car. He was so friendly I thought he was going to go with them. He probably would have, only they closed the car door real quick and told him they'd see him later.

As for me, I didn't get any further than the hall door. There was no need for me to. Da was doing well enough making a show of the

family without me adding to it. What was perfect was best left alone.

Ma didn't get to see the two boyfriends until the next time. She was out doing some late-night shopping. She felt nervous when she heard Fiona and Kathleen went off in a car with two fellows.

'They're not rough types?' she asked.

'No, they're pansies,' I told her.

'What time did they say they'd be back?' Ma asked Da.

'I forgot to ask.'

35

'D'you know what they work at?'

'They own a travel agency. Told me if I ever wanted a holiday they'd fix me up with a free trip.'

'That'd be nice.'

I thought it would be nice too. The best place for Da to go on a free holiday would be to Lourdes. He has this donkey laugh, meaning he laughs like a donkey. He's been to lots of doctors. He was even with a hypnotist. They all told him not to come back. He can't be cured.

'Da,' I said, 'why don't you ask those two lads to send you to Lourdes?'

He didn't like what I said. 'You tryin' to be cheeky?'

'Naw, jus' tryin' to help.'

I didn't say any more. Da was real sensitive about his donkey laugh. He wasn't the only one. We were too.

My two sisters came home at half-twelve. Ma was all over them, trying to find out what kind of lads they were out with.

I couldn't understand what she was worried

about. Anyone could see they were puffs. (That was a word Mad Victor picked up when he and Mad Henry were in the Home; you pick up a lot of useful information in places like that.) But you couldn't say that to Fiona and Kathleen, Ma nor Da, they thought they were great stuff altogether.

'Did they ask you out again?'

'Friday.'

Fiona and Kathleen; Theodore and Basil.

Theodore and Basil! That's what the two lads were called.

No wonder they found my sisters attractive. With names like that they'd find everyone attractive.

# 6 Bees' Knees United

The following Sunday we all met early for our match against Bees' Knees United. It was an away game. We didn't like them much. They didn't like us either, especially their manager. He was kind of stuck-up, in the sense that he thought his team was too good to step out on the same pitch as us. Five of his team were on the Dublin Schoolboys panel; that meant they were all in with a chance of getting on the Irish Schoolboys team during the season.

Us, we were on nothing; nor were we ever likely to be. That's except maybe for Chippy, but in a way he was too much of his own man to be on any panel. We knew only too well that Bees' Knees United thought they were way above us, but we didn't care. We had our new minibus to travel in, and we had a new football strip Harry Hennessy had got from Guinness. He wrote them a begging letter, at least Chippy said it was a begging letter.

'It could have been worse, though,' croaked Mad Victor.

'Wha' d'ye mean?'

'It coulda been from the Vincent de Paul. Or the War On Want. I get loads of stuff from the War On Want.'

Mad Victor often got stuff from the War On Want. Once he got a fur coat that went all the way down to his ankles. The previous winter, when the snow and cold got real bad, he wore

it a few times to football training. We didn't see much of it after that. Then he put it on a holy statue in the school grounds. We waited for one of the teachers to kick up blue murder, but they were that thick they didn't cop on for days. Just when they spotted there was something odd about the statue, someone came along in a car and stole the coat.

Mrs O'Leary, our favourite oul' wan, wears a fur coat now and again. But we know her coat is not the one Mad Victor had stolen. Hers has a slight burn mark on the back where she once sat on an ash-tray by mistake. In case you don't know, Mrs O'Leary is on Bray Urban District Council. She's going great guns. She's driving all the other Councillors daft.

But she'll have no problem getting re-elected. Trouble is, no one else will want to sit on the Council with her, she nags so much. Next time around she'll have to run the Council on her own. Mrs O'Leary we hear about all the time. She has headlines in the local paper every week. She's given up on football though. She hates the sight of us. She won't even say hello, she'll cross the road before she'd do that. But she's still gunning for Mad Victor. She'll never forget Mad Victor. Who would?

Anyway, back to the match against Bees' Knees United. What really annoyed us about them was they were so full of themselves. They thought they should be up there with the likes of Spurs, Liverpool, Everton, the cream of the English Premiership. Us, we were just us, and that was what made matters worse.

While Mr Glynn and Harry Hennessy were wearing their ordinary clothes on the sideline, the Bees' Knees management were wearing track-suits and flash runners, and had a medical bag with all kinds of sprays, bandages and stuff in it. As for us, Riverside, although we all had the jerseys, nicks and socks we got from Mr Arthur Guinness, we had no track-suits like the Bees' Knees subs had while waiting for a chance to come on to the pitch. Our subs had no track-suits; only jumpers or jackets to stand around in.

And we were sure glad Mad Victor was playing and not a sub. Because if he was standing on the line he'd have made a real show of us. See, all his clothes have holes in them. They start in his shoes and go all the way up to his neck. He has that many holes in his clothes a rabbit would get lost in them.

The only department we could outmatch Bees' Knees United in was the half-time refreshments. They only had water, while we had Coke, Fanta and Seven-Up. Mr Glynn always brought large bottles of Coke, Fanta and Seven-Up to all the Riverside matches he was in charge of. And that started the trouble.

The first half had finished nil-all. Maybe Bees' Knees should have been a goal up, but we defended well. We played most of the team behind the ball, except for Flintstone. We just let him run around the place and do as he liked. But the rest of us, we wouldn't come out of our own half. We chased and thumped every Bees' Knees player soon as he got anywhere within thirty yards of our goal. That really upset them. Soon as the first half ended scoreless, we could see we had them rattled.

We made straight for the Coke, Fanta and

Seven-Up. It wasn't our fault the sun was splitting the heavens that day. The season had only begun and it was almost as warm as a scorching hot summer's day. No, it wasn't our fault we were as thirsty as hell from chasing the other team all over the pitch. The first few that got their hands on the bottles of Coke, Fanta and Seven-Up wouldn't let go. They kept gulping and gulping – that's until the bottles were pulled from them.

That's when the row started. We ended up all over the side-line fighting over the three bottles. There was nothing Mr Glynn, Harry Hennessy or the referee could do to stop the rowing, not until the last drop was drunk, the last wrestling match finished.

You could sense the Bees' Knees players were gloating. They were delighted to see us make a show of ourselves. I suppose that was what brought us to our senses, when we saw the mocking look in their eyes. That really united us again, and we were determined to hang on for the second half and maybe score a breakaway goal.

But that didn't happen. Instead, we got beaten 2-nil. We could have drawn, only the ref robbed us twice, and Chippy struck the cross-bar with a twenty-yard free-kick. The Bees' Knees manager was mad keen on Chippy. Every time Chippy got the ball your man's eyes lit up. Chippy was a class act, much better than any player Bees' Knees United had. They'd be after Chippy, try to get him to join them – only they wouldn't get him. Chippy was one of us, and that was that.

Mr Glynn gave out all the way back to Bray.

'You let the club down, fighting over the Fanta and Seven-Up. I wouldn't have minded if it was against anyone else ... but against that crowd!'

'I didn't get no Fanta or Seven-Up,' sulked Flintstone.

'You got plenty.'

'I got nothin'.'

'You got a black eye, didn't you.'

Flintstone had sure got a black eye.

'It's gone blind. I can't see nothin' with it.'

'That's because it's closed. It'll be all right in

the mornin' when the swellin' goes down.'

And it was all right, eventually. And when it was, Flintstone thought it was a miracle and went to confession. Only there was no priest in the confession box. That didn't stop him. He likes to talk to himself a lot. So he just sat there and talked, and listened.

Flintstone was good at telling confessions.

He could hear them too.

He stayed in the confessional an extra half an hour, but no one was interested.

After a while, Father Bourke came into the

45

church. Flintstone got out of the confession box in the nick of time.

'You're young McKay, aren't you?'

'Yes, Father.'

'Don't you think it's time to go home!'

'Why, wha' time is it?'

'Half six.'

Half six meant it would be twenty to seven by the time Flintstone would get home. Half six was tea-time. Flintstone hoped he wouldn't miss out. You have to be home rapid to get your tea in Flintstone's house.

'Father, who's the patron saint of black eyes?'

Father Bourke didn't bother answering. Just got Flintstone out and sent him home.

Father Bourke knows everyone who plays for Riverside. It isn't that he ever comes to see us play. Like Flintstone in the confession box, he just knows us, that's all.

# 7 Mrs O'Leary Sees Red

Now that the soccer season had started I was happy as Larry. The only upset was the fact that the computer was broken. I still hadn't brought it to the factory in Swords to try and get it fixed. The reason I didn't bother had nothing to do with laziness. It was because Brains O'Mahony had made arrangements for me to get computer lessons from his sister. She was a computer whizz-kid and knew computers inside out. I went to her a few times, but it got embarrassing. I couldn't get the hang of using a computer at all. I felt real thick. After a while, I gave up on computer lessons altogether. I even gave up on writing. Instead, I got out my new football boots and went mad playing soccer.

Already we'd won three matches. One was against Rosemount from Dundrum. Their pitch is just across the road from Rosemount estate. There are a few pitches really, with a high wall at the back. The wall is as high as a house, impossible to climb. Mad Victor got curious when he saw the wall.

'Wha's that?' he asked.

'A wall, dopey.'

'I know it's a wall. Why is it so high? Wha's it belong to?'

'It's Dundrum Mental Hospital. They have to have the wall like that, so as no one can get out.'

Mad Victor didn't wait to hear any more. He walked straight off the pitch and hid in the back of the minibus until the match was over. No amount of coaxing could get him to come out, but we won without him anyway.

'Don't ever bring me to tha' place again,' Mad Victor kept on saying on the way home to Bray. 'Don't ever!'

Mad Victor has a fear of places with high walls. Only lately, Mrs O'Leary had Victor and his little brother, Mad Henry, sent away to a Home, but they escaped. Mrs O'Leary hadn't given up on catching them either. She was often around the estate searching for them.

But she was afraid to come near our football pitch any more, because we'd only run her off. Mrs O'Leary is real nosey. Lately, someone's been slagging her by writing comments on walls around the town. She thinks it's Mad Victor. But it's not. It's probably someone else. It's probably Chippy that's doing all the writing on the walls.

He denies doing it, but there's a fair chance it's him. Chippy's sly, sly enough to con Mrs O'Leary.

Although we'd won our last three games, Mr Glynn and Harry Hennessy made us train an extra night a week. Not that we wanted to, but Mr Glynn said he would bring us on a trip to London in April if we trained hard and our results picked up. We felt good about the idea, because a trip to London would be almost as good as a trip to Mars, once we got back.

All our normal training was in the People's Park, but the extra night was to be on Bray sea front. The idea was to tog out in the shelters, but winter came early, so we used the back of

Mr Glynn's minibus.

Some of us used to go to the sea-front training session early and we'd play poker, maybe have a sing-song to pass the time before the others showed up.

Sometimes Victor would bring his little brother, Mad Henry, and after the poker game he'd act as a ball-boy, whenever the ball would go into the sea or out on to the road. Sometimes he'd even stand in as a spare goal-post, if need be.

Chippy is a real poker shark. None of us can outsmart him at poker. He always showed up early. Most of the time we couldn't see the way he was dealing the cards in the dark, and we'd have to run out of the shelter, over to the street light, to see how our cards were shaping up. But Chippy very seldom went over to the light. He probably has cat's eyes. If the trip to London was ever to come off Chippy would have plenty of spending money saved from the poker games – our money!

We always finished the poker games before Mr Glynn arrived. He wasn't into poker, any form of gambling. Us, we loved it, horse-racing included. We know all about every horse, every race going. Mad Victor is an expert on horse-racing. If we ever want to back a horse we'd ask Mad Victor first. Even his uncles ask him first before they back a horse, and they're supposed to be experts.

Mad Victor's good with greyhounds too. But he doesn't like backing them, because he says the races are all fixed. One of his uncles owned a few greyhounds once, but he got banned because he was bringing over other greyhounds from England and racing them in his own greyhounds' names. Greyhound-racing is definitely dodgy. Maybe Chippy should become a greyhound-trainer. He'd do well.

When we trained on the sea front, we played more football than anything else. We always gave the flower-beds a real good hammering, and left a few skid-marks on the grass lawns. Harry Hennessy was the worst for skid marks. He liked to play football with us. His favourite was sliding tackles, only his weight fairly dug the place up, especially when it rained.

We didn't mind Harry playing with us, once we kept out of his way. The way we looked at it was, once Harry was enjoying himself we didn't want to spoil his fun. The only worry we had was we were afraid he might have a heart attack. With his weight, it would be no joke trying to lift him off the ground and cart him off to hospital. No, if that happened we'd just ring for an ambulance and let them get on with the job.

Not that we don't like Harry; we're all mad about him. It's just that heart attacks aren't our scene, that's all. Heart attacks are for doctors and nurses to look after, not us. If it was left to us Harry wouldn't have a chance. One thing though, we all know the number to ring if Harry ever does have a heart attack. What's more we always hold back the exact change for the phone call. If that's not being considerate, nothing is. Nobody can say that we don't care about Harry Hennessy. We do. Only for us he'd be lost.

Mrs O'Leary wasn't long in finding out

about us training on Bray sea front. She'd gone down there for a walk with some of her grandchildren one Sunday afternoon.

She saw all the skid marks, the flower-beds trampled on, the bare spots where the grass had gone patchy. She got talking to this oul' wan who told her about us wrecking the place with our football practice.

'Is that so?' she said.

'Yes, that's so.'

'And who would they be?'

'I couldn't say for certain. But this fat man is

always with them. And the other man has a van.'

'The van, is it blue?'

'Yes, a blue van. The fat man is the worst of all. Never stops shouting and cursing. He's a disgrace, showing that kind of example to the kids. Mind you, they aren't much better themselves. They're a very rowdy lot.'

'Did you catch any of their names?'

'I think I heard them call the fat man Harry. There's another who's called Chippy. And an absolutely revolting brat called Victor.'

Mrs O'Leary's eyes lit up when she heard the name Victor. Straight away she got excited and swung her handbag, just missing one of the grandchildren by inches.

'I know them! What nights are they here?'

'Tuesdays, I think. I'm not certain, but I'll let you know.'

And the oul' wan did let Mrs O'Leary know. We found out one Tuesday when it was too wet to train. It was absolutely teeming rain, so Mr Glynn called training off. In case some of us hadn't been told he went to the sea front around training time. He didn't bother bringing the van. He went in his car instead. None of us were there, but the guards were. They were in a squad-car. They only hung around for a short while before going off somewhere else, leaving a young garda near where we train – just in case we showed up.

When the garda noticed Mr Glynn in the car he asked if he could sit in so as to keep out of the wet. He hadn't a clue who Mr Glynn was because he was watching out for a van, not a car. So he told him all about what he was up to, mainly that he was there because Mrs O'Leary had made a complaint about lads playing football on the sea front. Only he didn't mention Mrs O'Leary; he said it was a Councillor that complained.

'A Councillor complained, did he?'

'Yes, only it was a woman Councillor.'

'A woman?'

'A Mrs O'Leary.'

Mr Glynn didn't hang around. He drove straight off, saying he had to get some petrol for a trip to Cork. He said he'd give the garda a lift up the town, that's if he wanted one. But, being young and green, the garda was full of enthusiasm, so he got out of the car and stood in the rain.

And that's how we found out it was Mrs O'Leary. Anyway, we should have known. Because Mrs O'Leary always interferes. She's the biggest interferer in Bray. The only time her interfering did any good was when some lad clipped the wings of the young ducks on the Dargle. The idea was that by Christmas the ducks would be well fattened. On account of having clipped wings they'd be easily caught, just in time for a good feed. Mrs O'Leary found out and the lad was caught. He got sent away, and we were all glad. But I bet Mrs O'Leary wished it had been Mad Victor. She really hates Mad Victor. She shouldn't, because Mad Victor's not bad; he's good, once you get to know him.

That finished all training on Bray sea front. Not that we were upset. We just hoped it wouldn't put an end to the trip to London. But we needn't have worried. Mr Glynn got us another place that was well lit where we could train on a Tuesday night, so that put the trip to London back on course.

We didn't forget Mrs O'Leary though. Some of us still went down the sea front, but never on a Tuesday. We varied the night so as not to get caught. Sometimes we'd head off in our football gear. We'd let her see us. We knew she'd follow us. Then, when we'd get to the sea front, with her after us, we'd be nowhere to be seen. Sometimes she'd have the guards and the Beautiful Bray Association there too. We gave her such a hard time that, in the end, she got fed up following us. We gave up on the sea front completely after that.

Mrs O'Leary, Councillor, tyrant, pain in the neck.

# 8 The Birthday Party

Just after our run in with Mrs O'Leary my sister Fiona had her birthday. One of the pubs over our way, which is closed down, has a disco and my da asked the owner could we use it for a party. He said we could. Ma brought plenty of food for everyone to eat, Da kind of paid a DJ to look after the music. The whole estate went, including Theodore and Basil, my sisters' boyfriends. But my sisters wouldn't let any of my pals in, especially Mad Victor and his little brother Henry. They had to stand outside in the rain and let on what was going on inside the disco.

I was disgusted. So I stayed outside in the hall with Joey Ryan, who's the bouncer for the disco when it's open. After a while, we let Mad Victor and Henry into the hallway and sneaked them some food. Joey bought them a glass of Coke each. Mad Victor and Henry were soaked from the rain, but they didn't mind once they got a bite to eat and a glass of Coke. What was more, Mad Victor was a real good disco dancer, better than what was inside at the party.

He tried to get Henry to dance, but Henry wouldn't. He said he didn't like discomusic.

'Jigs 'n' reels,' he said.

'What d'ye mean?'

'I only do Irish dancin'.'

'He's medals at home for boxin' an' Irish dancin'.'

'You have?'

'Yeah, I love Irish dancin'. That disco stuff is crap.'

And it would stay crap. There'd be no jigs and reels at my sister's party.

'Just as well you're not in there, then. They'd only laugh at you doin' Irish dancin' in a disco.'

'That's wha' ye think. That's where the boxin' comes in handy.'

Joey Ryan, the bouncer, really took a shine to Mad Victor and Henry. There was a room, off the hallway, full of chairs, coat-hangers and stuff. He knew Victor and Henry were short of furniture at home, so he put a proposition to them.

'The fella who owns this place is sellin' out. The new owner'll only throw everythin' out an' bang in all new stuff. Why don't you take home a few things for the house?'

Mad Victor and Henry didn't have to be asked a second time. They loaded up and made four or five trips backwards and forwards from the disco.

As for me, that's how I got the small table

and swivel-chair that's in the box-room at home. They'll come in useful if I ever get back writing again.

It might have been my sister's birthday, but in a way it was ours as well. Mine and Mad Victor and Henry's.

We didn't feel as if we were robbing anything, not if it all was going to be thrown out.

Neither did we feel as if we were being given it for nothing – we had to go to the bother of carrying it home. What with the rain and all.

Happy birthday, Fiona!

Happy birthday, everybody!


Talking of Fiona, she and Kathleen were getting on great with Basil and Theodore, their new boyfriends. Already they had taken Fiona and Kathleen out three times. That was a record, an all-time record. Only for Heather McFadden, my ex-flame, turning them into powdered beauties they'd still be full-time at home, darning the holes in Da's socks and playing Oasis records. Only for the fact I was going with Heather McFadden at the time my sisters would still be as plain as ever. Now that she had shown them how to use make-up, they looked as exciting as Sharon Stone. And I knew it would last, once they didn't stay out in the rain too much.

Mentioning Heather McFadden, she was going with a fellow from Blackrock College now. He's a rugby player with half a cauliflower ear and a twisted nose. I don't know what she sees in him. He doesn't even speak properly. He's another puff, just like Basil and Theodore. Me and Heather McFadden are definitely finished. She doesn't even come to see us play any more. Instead she goes to Blackrock rugby matches. The only way I'd get back with her would be to grow two feet overnight and turn into James Dean. Heather McFadden is mad about James Dean. Only thing: James Dean is dead, nothing can bring him back. Only Jesus can do that. Hard luck, James Dean. Hard luck, me.

I tried to do some writing the other day. I

was going to write a poem and send it to Heather McFadden. Just as I got going Basil and Theodore came up into the room. They were waiting to take Fiona and Kathleen out and were trying to keep away from Da, that's why they came up to the box-room.

'Didn't know you wrote?' said Basil.

'Well, you know now.' I was kind of vexed, because they came across me unawares and I was in the middle of my soppy love poem to Heather McFadden, and I didn't want anybody seeing me writing a soppy love poem. So I blocked the poem with my hands.

'See you have a computer,' said Theodore.

'Yeah, only it doesn't work.'

'How's that?'

'It's banjaxed.'

'How long is it like that?'

'Ever since it fell on its head.'

'You let it fall?'

'No, I kicked it.'

'Why did you kick it?'

'I felt like it.'

Basil and Theodore said they knew a lot

about computers. They said they'd bring it with them and get it fixed. At first I wouldn't give it to them. But when they said they'd get it fixed for nothing I handed it over. They went downstairs and put it in their car.

'When'll I get it back?'

'About three weeks.'

Three weeks would do me fine. Three weeks I'd have it back and maybe this time I'd become a computer whizz-kid.

Three weeks.

I thought no more of it and got back to working on my soppy love poem to Heather McFadden.

# 9 Home Farm

Early in December, we played a crucial All-Ireland Cup game away to a team from Whitehall on the northside of Dublin. The team was Home Farm. Ten of their players were already on the Dublin Schoolboys panel. Most of them had been offered trials with top English Premiership clubs, and it was known that big-time scouts went to most of their games. Home Farm were easily the best team in Dublin and we were quaking in our boots at what the score would be.

The first we knew of drawing Home Farm in the All-Ireland Cup was about three weeks before we played them. We didn't feel too bad when Mr Glynn first gave us the news, but by the time the game came around we were completely freaked out with nerves, that's all except Flintstone, and that was only because, unbelievably, he'd never heard of Home Farm in his life.

'Home Farm, who're they?'

'The best team goin'.'

'Never heard of them.'

'You will, after they hammer us ten-nil.'

'Wha' are they, farmers?'

'Naw, the best football team in Ireland.'

It was all right for Flintstone. He could only count to five; after that he wouldn't have a clue. But the rest of us, we knew we'd get walloped.

All of a sudden we didn't want to go.

'Call the match off, Mr Glynn.'

'What?'

'Call it off.'

'We can't do that.'

'Give them a walkover then. Tell them Harry Hennessy died and we have to go to his funeral.'

'That's no attitude to have. They're only flesh and blood.'

'They are not, Mr Glynn. They're Home Farm, the best team in the known world.'

'They're just like yourselves. Think positive and you could beat them.'

'The only chance we'd have of beatin' them would be if there was no referee an' the ground swallowed them all up after five minutes.'

'You can beat them.'

'No, we can't.'

The night before the game Mr Glynn and Harry Hennessy took us all to the pictures. Normally, when we go to the pictures we have great fun, but not this time. We were too nervous. The only thing that could settle us were a few fags. To do that we had to go out to the toilets, as Mr Glynn and Harry Hennessy were dead against us smoking. There were that many of us in the toilets that some oul' lad reported us to the management. An usher came in and put us out of the cinema. We were all gone home by the time Mr Glynn and Harry Hennessy knew there was anything wrong.

They came around to our houses later, making sure we were all right and that we'd show up for the match the next day. Harry Hennessy even offered to let us stay overnight in his house. Later we heard that he and Mr Glynn were worried we wouldn't show up at all. But they needn't have worried; we did.

We were as quiet as mice on the way into Dublin to Home Farm's football pitch. On the way, Mr Glynn read out the team. It was the one time I can ever remember wishing I wouldn't be on it. Usually, Mr Glynn didn't announce the team until we were in the dressing-rooms immediately before a game. I suppose he thought we might feel a bit more at ease if he told us earlier than usual. But it was a mistake. Soon as Growler Hughes heard his name mentioned he felt sick. Luckily, he was sitting next to a window. The car behind wasn't so lucky though. Growler gave it a splashing.

The team from one to eleven was:

1 – Noel Moore: he's our goalkeeper. We call him 'The Octopus', he seems to have that many extra hands. Not when he's playing football, but when he goes into the shops.

2 – Simon Nolan: the best right-full in Bray. Only problem, he's left-footed.

3 – Ray Heaney: our left-full. He likes to slog the ball. Good in the tackle though. Anyone he tackles ends up in the same place as the ball – over the side-line.

4 – Studs Mooney: he plays at the centre of the defence, alongside Growler Hughes. He's small and mean, likes to show his studs. That's why he's nicknamed 'Studs'.

5 – Growler Hughes: he's our centre-half. Always moaning and giving out. Still, a good centre-half.

6 – John O'Brien: that's Chippy. Star player. Plays centre-midfield.

7 – Jimmy Quinn: that's me. Outside-right or right-midfield. Better than most of the other players. At least I say I am.

8 – Nigger Doyle: kind of old-fashioned inside-right. No one knows why he's called 'Nigger'. He's as white as a packet of Surf.

9 – Victor Costello: that's Mad Victor. Centre-forward. But he ends up all over the place. He doesn't score many goals. Chippy scores most of those.

10 – Sean Holden: centre-midfield with

Chippy. Clever type of player. Too clever for most of us.

11 – David McKay: outside-left. David McKay is Flintstone. He's not very good at kicking a ball, but he can run all day. Worth having, because when he's playing the opposition doesn't know what's going on.

Home Farm is a big club, with pitches all over the place. By the time we found the right one the players were already out on the pitch, ready for the kick-off. Mr Glynn and Harry Hennessy rushed us into the dressing-rooms to get togged out. Maybe it was good in the end that everything ended up in a rush. We hadn't time to think about Home Farm and our nerves kind of settled. Before we knew it, we were out on the pitch; the game was on.

We were 2-0 down after ten minutes. But gradually Chippy clawed us back into the game, and it still was only 2-0 at half-time. What's more, we could have scored, only Mad Victor took a dive in the penalty area when he was clean through. He claimed he was tripped, but there was no one near him, not even the goal-keeper.

We gave Victor some lashing at half-time. Maybe the lashing didn't do Victor much good, but it boosted our ego no end. We actually felt as if we could score a goal in the second half. And Home Farm hadn't finished the half as well as they started it. Looking back, I think they got afraid of us. Who could blame them, what with the likes of Mad Victor, Growler Hughes and Studs Mooney to contend with. And then there was Chippy. Chippy was pure class, head and shoulders above the rest of us. He was even better than the best of the Home Farm players.

When we went out for the second half we noticed three oul' lads on the side-line. Mr Glynn said they were the selectors for Dublin Schoolboys. He told us if we played well we might get on the U-15 team. We were worse eejits to believe him. We played our hearts out. We tried that hard we were almost as good as Home Farm. But that didn't stop them getting a third goal and winning 3-0. Only for Mad Victor blowing his top and getting sent off, we probably would have done a lot better. Nearly worse than getting sent off, he went over to the three oul' lads who were selectors and gave them a right going-over.

'I was only doin' me best,' he shouted. 'I was only tryin' to impress, maybe get picked for yer rotten league team. If yous hadn't been here it woulda never happened, an' I wouldn't a got sent off. It's all your fault. Only for yous we mighta won!'

The three oul' lads weren't impressed. But they were with Chippy. After the match they went over to Mr Glynn and Harry Hennessy.

'We like the look of your number 6. What's his name?'

'John O'Brien.'

'We'd like another look. Any chance of sendin' him for squad-trainin'?'

'When?'

'Next Thursday night. At Home Farm's main pitch, across the road from the Regency Airport Hotel.'

'What time?'

'Half seven.'

'What are his chances?'

'Well, if he shapes up as well as he did here, he could get in.'

Mr Glynn liked that bit. So too did Harry Hennessy. They'd do their best to have Chippy available for Thursday night, even if they had to bring him into Dublin themselves.

On the way home in the minibus, Mr Glynn told us what the three oul' selectors had to say.

'Was no one else asked in for trainin' on Thursday night?' queried Growler.

'No.'

'I'm not surprised. Them three oul' lads are pure dopes. I took three shots off the line. They should know any centre-half tha' clears three shots off the line is good. I shoulda at least gotta mention.'

'You got a mention all right.'

'I did?'

'Yeah. You're going to be up before the League committee.'

'Wha' d'ya mean?'

'When Victor got sent off, he gave your name.'

Growler did his nut. Next thing, we all went spare, wrestling and acting the fool in the back of the minibus. Straight away we forgot about Home Farm and being knocked out of the All-Ireland Cup. That was one thing about us; when it came to losing we had short memories.

Chippy was quiet enough, he didn't mess.

When he got home he went straight to his ma, and said, 'Ma, I'm goin' to be on the Dublin Schoolboys team.'

And he would. That much was a certainty.

# 10  Chippy Makes It

Chippy got on the Dublin Schoolboys panel, no bother. That meant, as of now, Chippy was famous, because sometimes the panel was listed in the *Evening Herald* on a Tuesday night, saying when training and special matches were on. Each player's club was listed beside his name. Beside Chippy's name, in brackets, it gave 'Riverside Boys'. In a way, it made us all feel kind of famous. Everyone who plays for Riverside likes to see their name in print, me included. That's one of the reasons I want to be a writer. That way I'll always be in print. Footballers come and go. Writers are forever.

The only one of us who's always in print is Growler Hughes. Well, not Growler directly, but his da, who is also called Growler.

Growler Senior is always before the courts, meaning he gets a mention in the local paper every week. He is very fond of the Dargle river; that's because he likes poaching salmon. Sometimes he poaches from the river bank, other times he gets into the river and helps himself.

Once I saw him in the river opposite Bray Golf Club. He had a bucket in one hand and a gaff-hook hidden inside the flap of his jacket.

'Wha' ya doin', Growler?'

'Lookin' for golf balls.'

Yes, Growler's da is nearly always in the local paper. Seeing his name is like following a TV serial, with different episodes each week. A week without Growler's da in the paper is a week lost.

Studs Mooney's da is also in the *Bray People* most weeks. Just like Studs is mean on the football pitch, his da is mean off it. He is something of a con man. Most of us don't like Studs's da, because if he thinks we have any money he asks for a loan, especially from Chippy, Flintstone and me when we're doing our vegetable round. One house we always keep away from is Studs's, because we know his oul' lad would do us up to the eyeballs.

Talking of fathers, Flintstone's da is a real oddball. He's Celtic mad. He's that mad about Celtic, sometimes he tries to speak with a Scottish accent, but he's as Bray as can be. Like Flintstone, he's soft in the head. He wears a Celtic jersey night and day. But when winter comes he wears it as a vest. It reappeared last summer as a football jersey. Now it's gone again, probably a vest. By next summer it'll be in tatters. He'll have to start saving to buy a new one. Flintstone's da finds it hard to save. He finds it hard to do anything.

Getting back to Chippy and the Dublin Schoolboys panel: it meant that for some games we were going to lose out having him on our team, because he'd have to go away with the Dublin Schoolboys and play against other representative teams.

One such game was against North Wales in a place called Conway. He had a great time, even brought back some presents. He gave me and Mad Victor one. He gave Harry Hennessy a pint-glass with a dragon engraved on the side. Harry was delighted.

'Wha's this?' he asked.

'It's for you.'

'Wha's the dragon?'

'It's a Welsh dragon. They're into dragons in Wales. Only thing, there's none there.'

Mad Victor was delighted with his present. It looked like a fish-bowl, only it wasn't. It was a bowl for trifle, but to Victor it looked like what a spaceman would wear over his head.

'I'll give it to me little brother Henry.'

'Why?'

'He can wear it to the pictures Sundays an'

let on he's goin' to Mars.'

Henry always goes to the pictures on Sunday afternoons. He goes with lots of little lads who live around our way. Although he is older than most of them he loves going with them. They all think the world of him. They regard him as their leader. Like Victor, Henry isn't completely mad. He collects all the picture money off the little lads outside the door and buys all the tickets together. Then he gets them running all around the place so as they can't be counted. That way, Henry gets in for nothing. Usually, once inside they quieten, except when the hero comes on screen.

Chippy brought back other presents too. Plenty of towels and pillow-cases. RH was stamped on the towels.

'Wha's RH, Chippy?'

'The initials of the hotel we stayed in.'

'Ye mean, ye nicked them?'

'Yeah.'

'An' the bowl, the pint-glass?'

'They're souvenirs ye know. Everyone takes stuff from hotels. It's expected of you.'

The week-end Chippy was away with the Dublin Schoolboys in Wales we were down to play a team from Dominick Street in Dublin. They weren't going too well in the League. In fact, they were two off the bottom. We had to play them in the Phoenix Park, which was just as well as there was a mob of them. They had only won one match all season, but that didn't stop them from showing up. Usually when a team is doing badly they struggle to field a team, but not this lot. They were mad keen to get dug into us.

Five minutes gone, they scored against us. They had this big centre-forward, Rommel they called him. He glanced the ball into our net with as nifty a header as I've ever seen. His mates went berserk, hugging and kissing him. One even kissed the ball before it was replaced on the centre-circle. They knocked lumps out of us after that. We ended up getting beaten 3-2, Rommel scoring a hat-trick.

We felt real bad on the way home. There wasn't any of the usual singing, any remarks shouted out of the minibus window. Instead, we all sat in complete misery. We knew exactly why we'd got beaten. It wasn't because we had played badly. It wasn't because we hadn't tried hard enough. It was because we hadn't Chippy. Chippy was the one who gelled us together. Without Chippy we weren't the same.

As of then, we began to curse the Dublin Schoolboys team, Chippy included.

We began to dread any time the Dublin Schoolboys U-15 team would have a match, because without Chippy we'd probably get beaten.

Not that there were that many matches left. But it brought home to us the fact that without Chippy we were clueless.

What's more, we knew we couldn't hold on to him forever. That some day he'd leave. Even Bees' Knees United were eyeing him. They all were.

No, we knew someday we'd lose Chippy.

When that would happen we'd be finished.

I sent my love poem off to Heather McFadden.

I sent it by post in a pink envelope. Apart from the poem, I hadn't written anything in ages. I felt real proud of it. I felt it was that good Heather McFadden couldn't but be affected by it. She was affected all right. She sent it back along with a note telling me to get lost. That totally finished me with Heather McFadden. She even moved to a posh school.

I didn't see her any more, except once I saw her photo in the *Irish Independent* hugging some rugby freak from Blackrock College after they won the Leinster Senior Cup. The freak's mother was on one side, Heather on the other, the Leinster Senior Cup in the middle. That photo nearly broke my heart, but I got over it. Eventually.

Heather McFadden wasn't the only person I didn't see any more. Basil and Theodore went missing along with my computer. Da went to the travel agency they ran, but when he got there it wasn't a travel agency but some fancy pub where yuppies hung out. There wasn't a trace of Basil or Theodore, or wouldn't be. The only certainty was the money they got for flogging my computer.

Da kept going on about Basil and Theodore, but the barmen told him to get out.

'Get out, or we'll get the law.'

'That,' bawled Da in disgust, '… that is justice?'

Da got out, but not until he cursed the barmen and yuppie law from a height.

I wasn't the only one who never saw Basil or Theodore again. My two sisters never saw them either. Overnight they turned into man-haters. Even the sight of a tom-cat in the garden drove them into a rage.

'Birds of a feather flock together,' said my ma.

I nodded my head in agreement.

'What's more, they fly off together.'

Basil and Theodore. Like Butch Cassidy and the Sundance Kid they were gone to pastures new.

# 11  Blessed Oliver

Chippy wasn't the only one we stood to lose off our football team. Just short of Christmas Mad Victor and Henry were up Bray Main Street singing carols when they ran foul of Mrs O'Leary. Mrs O'Leary thought they were begging, but all they were doing was singing *Jingle Bells* and *Rudolph the Red-Nosed Reindeer*. What happened was, when they saw Mrs O'Leary they became kind of dumbstruck and weren't able to sing. They had this fear of Mrs O'Leary because lately she'd been going around the town looking for them because she wanted to send them to a Home in Dun Laoghaire. On account of them having no parents, and living with their uncles who were always drunk, she thought it the proper thing to do.

When Mrs O'Leary saw Victor and Henry holding a cardboard box to put money in, she naturally thought they were begging. The sight was like waving a red flag in front of a bull. Only Mrs O'Leary wasn't a bull, because a bull can't shout and make a show of people. She flayed at Victor and Henry with her handbag. But they took off up the laneway at the Arcade and out into the car park at the back of the Holy Redeemer Church.

They hid under a car and could see Mrs O'Leary's fat legs going by. They gave her a few minutes, got over a wall into Brighton Terrace, back to the top of the Main Street, where they stood with cupped hands singing carols outside the Bank of Ireland.

Seeing Mad Victor and Henry committing so-called begging was the last straw as far as Mrs O'Leary was concerned. Now that she was big-time with Bray Urban District Council she dreaded to think what kind of image they would create for the town. Maybe there would be an epidemic of begging. No, she'd have to round up Mad Victor and Henry and have them sent away to a Home. She'd have to have the problem sent away somewhere else, as far away from Bray as possible.

Mrs O'Leary went to their house. She got social workers, health officials, everything short of nuns, around too. But Victor and Henry were never there. Neither were their uncles. They were all on the run.

And where did Mad Victor and Henry stay when on the run? Mostly in carriages beside Bray railway station. But on really frosty nights they stayed with Harry Hennessy. Harry was very good to them. He gave them breakfast, dinner and tea, everything short of letting them drink his Guinness.

We knew once Mrs O'Leary caught up with Mad Victor and Henry it would only be hours before they'd be sent away. The team wouldn't be the same without Victor, its heart would be taken away.

What with Chippy maybe going too, it was looking like the end of the road.

Christmas week we had a great time. Chippy was picked for the Dublin Schoolboys team against Belfast. The game was to be played in Drogheda. We all wanted to see Chippy play because Mr Glynn said he'd bring us in the minibus and treat us to a day out. The only upset was we'd miss out on the vegetable round, so we got Mad Henry and a few of his pals to fill in while we went to the match.

We should have known better. Mad Henry and his pals ended up throwing tomatoes at the oul' wans going up the town to do their shopping. They hid behind a wall, but the guards came along and took our wheelbarrow to the barracks as evidence. Only for Chippy's da being friendly with the law we would have never got it back.

Talking of the match against Belfast, we got to Drogheda early, that's all except Chippy, he travelled with the Dublin Schoolboys team. To kill some time, Mr Glynn brought us into this big church. There were lots of steps outside it, that many you could break a leg thirty times over.

'Mr Glynn, we don't want to say prayers.'

'Don't worry, we're not going in to say prayers.'

'Wha's the point of goin' in, then?'

'There's something in there I want to show you.'

And there was. There was some oul' lad's head.

'Where's the rest of him?' asked Mad Victor.

We gathered around and had a good look at the head. Some of us wanted to touch it, only it was in a glass case.

'Whose head is it, Mr Glynn?'

'Read the inscription.'

There was all this writing, explaining who the head belonged to. But it went on a bit, so we just read the piece about him being a bishop and getting his head cut off by the English.

'That's Blessed Oliver Plunkett's head.'

'I wouldn't call him "Blessed", Mr Glynn. I'd call him unfortunate.'

So would we all.

Mr Glynn told us all about Blessed Oliver Plunkett, better than any school-teacher would. By the time he finished we were all on our knees saying the Rosary and vowing we'd get our own back on the English for what they

did to Blessed Oliver Plunkett.

It ended up we couldn't get Blessed Oliver Plunkett off our minds, even when we went for a feed of chips before the match. At the match it got so bad that Mad Victor thought half the Dublin Schoolboys team looked like Blessed Oliver Plunkett.

'He looks like Blessed Oliver Plunkett, doesn't he?'

'Naw, he doesn't.'

'Well, yer man, then. He does, doesn't he?'

'Give off, Victor!'

Some of the managers from our League were at the match. We said hello, but they didn't want to know us. We were used to that kind of carry on. We just sniggered and passed a few smart remarks. We're all very good at passing smart remarks, especially Growler Hughes; he's pure genius. If you're ever short of a smart remark just go to Growler and he'll tell you one, no bother.

Bees' Knees United's manager was also at the match. He talked a little to Mr Glynn and Harry Hennessy. But he was dead against us. His name is Gerry Lowe. He's six-foot-four. If he was any taller he'd be well on his way to being the biggest eejit in Ireland. We have a nickname for him – 'High-Lowe' we call him. He works for Irish Lights in Dun Laoghaire. Chippy says he's a back-up lighthouse.

We gave Chippy a big cheer soon as we saw him on the pitch. He looked more like what belonged to Liverpool or Arsenal, than what played football in Bray Park week in, week out. You'd think butter wouldn't melt in his mouth.

The Dublin Schoolboys team were first out on the pitch. We thought the two teams would come out together. But they didn't. The Belfast crew were playing smart. They were holding back in the dressing-rooms on purpose, trying to make the Dublin Schoolboys nervous by having to wait about on the pitch. But the Dublin Schoolboys seemed happy enough knocking a few balls about and having a right good warm-up. And why wouldn't they be, with most of their families and football managers watching and the likes of us giving them a good cheer from the main stand?

There was even a pipe band marching up and down the pitch, blowing bagpipes and thumping drums like mad.

When the Belfast team came out some of them made straight for the band, thinking they'd have a parade, while the others stood to one side, as if they were getting ready for a fight. Well, that's the way it looked to us, because we've seen that kind of carry on plenty of times on the telly. And that's what people from Belfast really like, even better than football. But the referee got the pipe band off the pitch as quickly as he could and got the match going.

Soon as he blew the whistle the Belfast lads forgot all about pipe bands and parades and remembered who they were, eleven lads from the North who had to get stuck into the South. And our lads forgot all about their petty differences and remembered who they were, eleven lads from the South who had to get stuck into the North.

The first twenty minutes was played at break-neck speed. But gradually it slowed and Chippy came more into the game. He was playing centre-midfield. He began to hold the ball, stroking it about, dictating the trend of the game. Every pass he made was exact, every tackle clean and crisp.

'Who's yer man?'

'He's from Bray.'

'Bray?'

'Yeah, Bray.'

'Not one of that Riverside crowd?'

'Yeah.'

'Where did they get a player like that?'

'Don't know.'

No joking, that's the way the watching managers were going on about Chippy. We could hear them real plain. You'd think we'd no right to have a player as good as Chippy. It made us feel as if there was something wrong with us – as if we'd no right to be in their League, that we were only a crowd of nut-cases and rowdies. We could see for definite now the top Dublin managers would have a real dog-fight trying to land Chippy for their clubs. It was poaching season as far as Chippy was concerned.

The whole buzz at half-time was the way Chippy was playing.

It was the same after the game, they were all inviting Chippy to train with them. He didn't know what to say. Some of them even offered him a lift back to Dublin. But he went home with us in the minibus. He told Mr Glynn and Harry Hennessy all about the other teams asking him to train with them.

'They did?'

'Yeah.'

'How many?'

'The lot.'

Mr Glynn and Harry Hennessy were both fuming.

'I'll report them to the League.'

'But they *are* the League,' ranted Harry Hennessy. 'Report them to UEFA.'

'I'll pull him out of the Dublin Schoolboys team, that's what I'll do.'

'Pull him out?'

'Yeah, pull him out,' we all said.

'But that wouldn't be fair on Chippy. Chippy, what do you think?'

'Dunno.'

But Chippy did know. He didn't want to be pulled out.

We had murder over it all the way back to Bray. High-Lowe, the lot, were only a crowd of thieving poachers. We called them every name under the sun.

For the record, the Dublin Schoolboys won 1-nil. Chippy didn't score the goal, but he made it; he was the difference between the two teams, the best player on the pitch.

Unknown to us, early in the second half, Mad Victor had asked Mr Glynn for the keys to the minibus, as he was starving and had left some sandwiches in the back.

Mr Glynn gave him the keys. Victor didn't come back for a quarter of an hour. He had no sandwiches, just a contented smile on his face.

On the way home to Bray, just outside Balbriggan, Victor took sixteen pairs of trousers and dropped them one by one out of the minibus window.

'Who's trousers are they, Victor?'

'Don't know. But if they could speak they'd have Belfast accents.'

In a way, Victor had got his own back for what the English did to poor Blessed Oliver Plunkett. The lads from Belfast may not have been English, but in our minds they were at least half-English. And that was good enough for us. More than good enough as far as Victor was concerned.

Pity, he didn't take the Dublin Schoolboys' trousers as well.

That would have been perfect. A perfect end to a not-so-perfect day.

By the way, just for the record, I found out later that the Pope had made Blessed Oliver a saint – Saint Oliver.

For losing his head. Was it worth it?

# 12  Mrs O'Leary – Cow Rustler

Chippy was beginning to act up lately. When I told about what happened to the computer he went ape.

'That computer's worth two grand.'

'*Was*, it's gone. Anyway it was banjaxed.'

'Nothin' somebody in the know couldn't put right. How come ye handed it over to two strangers?'

'They weren't strangers, they were me sisters' boyfriends.'

'How am I to know ye're tellin' the truth? Ye probably flogged the computer an' kept the money for yerself.'

'I did not!'

'Maybe yer da did, then. Maybe he flogged the computer an' put the money on a nag.'

'He did not!'

'He tried to get at the money from the vegetable round, didn't he? After that he'd be up to anythin'.'

What Chippy said was true. Da had gone to the post-office and tried to get at our money from the vegetable round. He had been told of a sure winner, and our account was his only chance of getting a few quick bob. The clerk at the post-office wouldn't give him any money, told him to go home. Everybody in Bray knows about my da's addiction to horse-racing. He's a real embarrassment, my da, a real burden. Once he climbed up into a tree and wouldn't come down. We left him there. But the fire-brigade thought different. They took him down.

'I want a few bob compensation – half the money from the vegetable round.'

'Chippy, that's two hundred quid!'

'Well, that's what I want.'

'Chippy, it's not my fault. There's no way I should have to give you two hundred quid.'

'Well, don't give it to me. I'll just go to the post-office an' take it out myself.'

'You can't take it out by yourself, you have to have two signatures.'

'That's easily sorted out.'

'No, it's not. You'd only get into trouble.'

'Well, are ye goin' to sign for me, then?'

'No.'

Straight away Chippy knew I had him. Without my signature the money would have to stay put. But it caused trouble between us. We were rowing again. This time it could last.

Maybe some day I'll write a story about greed. If I do get round to it, Chippy would be a perfect example.

Something big happened in Bray on St Stephen's Day that took Mrs O'Leary's mind off tracking down Mad Victor and Henry. Most of Bray's Town Hall is a McDonald's restaurant. All the kids in Bray, even as far as Greystones and Wicklow, love going there. But Mrs O'Leary doesn't love McDonald's. She wouldn't mind if it were somewhere else. Anywhere, but not in the Town Hall, where upstairs she attends Bray Urban District Council meetings.

'McDonald's shouldn't be in the Town Hall, Jim. It should have never been allowed in the first place. D'ye hear me, Jim?'

Jim heard her all right. He couldn't help it. He's Mrs O'Leary's husband, a battered one at that. When out, he gets clouted with her handbag; in the house he gets clattered with a frying-pan; last thing at night he gets thumped with a hot-water bottle.

'The gall! Imagine, lettin' McDonald's into the Town Hall! Havin' that lovely buildin' turned into a fast-food chipper.' All the litter outside! The cars parked all over the place! All around the streets! All over private estates! It should never have been allowed! It should never have happened! Well, Jim O'Leary, what have you to say?'

Jim had nothing to say. Once he had, but not any more. It was safe to have nothing to say, that way Mrs O'Leary wouldn't batter him.

'Well, what have you to say …? What do you think …?'

'Nothin' really, Brenda.'

'Typical! Nothin'? Of course, it's somethin'! It's one of the biggest issues in this town and you say NOTHIN'!'

'What I mean, Brenda, nothin' can be done. It's too late, McDonald's are in the Town Hall now. They can't be put out.'

'We can try though. We can make one last attempt. It's not too late to march up there and make them leave.'

'Count me out, Brenda.'

'Count you out? You're comin' whether you like it or not.'

'But, Brenda …'

'You're comin'! The Town Hall belongs to the people of Bray, not McDonald's. Years ago farmers had fairs outside it. There were even dances there. The town was run from there. Don't forget when we were kids we played on the bales of sheeps' wool after it was weighed on the weigh-bridge at the back of the Town Hall. Remember all that, Jim O'Leary? Remember …?'

Jim remembered all right. In those days he was only a slip of a lad, Brenda a slip of a girl. She used to kiss him then. Not like now, all he got now was battered. Mad Victor says Jim O'Leary'd be better off a dog, that way people could report Mrs O'Leary to the Cruelty Against Animals and she'd be brought before the courts.

We all know who the dog was. Fortunately, it wasn't Jim.

'I'm startin' a campaign. I'll bring the matter up at the next council meetin'. If they don't do somethin', *I'll* march on McDonald's.'

And one day Mrs O'Leary *did* march on McDonald's. Soon as we got word we rushed to the Town Hall. Mrs O'Leary, along with her relatives and supporters, had already surrounded it. They had marched up the Main Street with lots of placards and a cow they had rustled from a field somewhere up Old Conna Avenue.

There was a placard tied to the cow's neck:

MAD COW
BEWEARE!

(That's how they spelt it, honest.)

Seemingly, they had stood outside the Town Hall for ages, chanting slogans and marching up and down. Mrs O'Leary wanted to see the

boss, but the boss didn't want to see her. Who could blame him? It was bad enough hearing her ranting about the Town Hall's heritage without having to go out and look her in the face. It would be worse than facing a raving Baluba from darkest Africa. No, there was no way the management was going to go out and talk.

In the end, Mrs O'Leary got fed up roaring. She opened the main door into McDonald's and shoved the cow inside.

That's when the fun really began. The staff

weren't too keen on the cow and they tried to shove it back outside. The cow got all muddled and began to knock Big Macs and milk shakes all over the place.

We were looking in at the windows. Flintstone was taking bets that the cow would pee on the floor. But it didn't. We could see Mrs O'Leary's crowd jostling with the staff, and she was letting fly with her handbag. A good few got thumped, especially the manager. He got it right in the face and went down like a ton of bricks.

Mrs O'Leary ended up chaining herself to the counter. She had a pair of handcuffs and told one of her crowd to go outside and throw the key down a drain.

The guards and all arrived, including a farmer to take the cow back home.

Mrs O'Leary had to wait a while longer. They had to use a hacksaw to get the handcuffs off her. When they did, they let her go home. That disappointed us, because we thought she'd be put in a squad-car and be taken to jail.

We think her husband was disappointed too. But he said nothing, just followed her home and got the tea ready.

It was a great laugh.

We're all hoping she'll march on McDonald's again.

So far nothing has happened.

But next time, if she does march, she'll be sent to jail and that will make a lot of people happy, especially us, the sons and daughters of Palermo. It'd be great seeing Mrs O'Leary in jail. Her husband wouldn't know himself, not getting nagged everyday.

Mrs O'Leary wouldn't know herself either, especially if she had to spend a few weeks in Mountjoy.

Fancy Mrs O'Leary being a jail-bird!

It'd be just great!

## 13 Growler's Master-stroke

We didn't see too much of Chippy after Christmas. He even went missing from the vegetable round. The first we knew of something being wrong was when we saw High-Lowe's car parked outside Mr Glynn's house. Seemingly Chippy had asked for a transfer. He said he wanted to leave Riverside and join Bees' Knees United.

'You what?'

'I wanna transfer.'

'Why? Why now, when everything is going so well? And you're on the Dublin Schoolboys team, and all that.'

'I'd be mixin' with a better class of player. I'd improve me chance of gettin' on the Irish Schoolboys team.'

'Better class of player? Growler's a better class of player.'

'Yeah, when he keeps his mouth shut. Anyway, I'd be better off joinin' Bees' Knees.

Plenty of their players always make the Irish Schoolboys panel.'

'Chippy, who's putting all these ideas into your head. It's High-Lowe, isn't it?'

Chippy didn't answer, not directly. But Mr Glynn knew it was High-Lowe. He was always snooping around trying to poach the cream of the crop. The same as a lot of managers do when trying to strengthen their teams.

Mr Glynn did his best to hold on to Chippy. But there wasn't a whole lot he could do when High-Lowe knocked at his door with a transfer form in his hand. What was more, the transfer dead-line was only a few days away.

Luckily, when we saw High-Lowe's car parked outside Mr Glynn's house we got straight on the phone to Mr Glynn to find out what was going on.

Right away Growler came up with a master-stroke of an idea. Most people only knew Chippy by his nickname, and although Chippy's real name had been in the *Evening Herald* a few times for Dublin Schoolboys panels, there was a good chance High-Lowe only knew Chippy by his nickname. Growler told Mr Glynn to take his time with High-Lowe while he'd go to Harry Hennessy and get a blank transfer form. He'd go straight over to Mr Glynn's house, knock on the door, get invited inside, switch the blank transfer form with High-Lowe's and send him on his way. Only the blank transfer form wouldn't be blank any more. It would have been made out in the name *James* O'Brien, not *John* O'Brien, signatured and all by Growler.

Growler's plan worked to a tee. High-Lowe took the false form and had it in the post inside the hour. He was delighted. So were we. We didn't say a word to anyone, especially not to Chippy. With the transfer dead-line only a few days away, one careless word would have ruined the plan.

We had to explain it all to Flintstone.

'Wha's the point? Chippy's signed the form – so he's gone.'

'But he didn't sign it, dope. Growler did. And the name on it is wrong. Chippy is "John", not "James".'

'So wha'?'

'So Chippy hasn't transferred to Bees' Knees. He can come back to us once the dead-line is past.'

'But he's not comin' back. He wants to leave us.'

'He can change his mind, Flintstone.'

But Flintstone had put his finger on the weak point of the plan. It would only work if Chippy wanted to come back to Riverside. Did he? And did we want him back? The notion of his wanting to leave us and join Bees' Knees made us feel kind of disgusted. Especially the fact of him thinking being a Riverside player would lessen his chances of getting on the Irish Schoolboys team. It was as if there was something wrong with us, as if we were lepers.

It made some of us feel so bad we went home and asked our mothers what was wrong with us. It was that daft, but still we felt very hurt. It was all right for Mad Victor, he was used to that kind of thinking, but not the rest of us, it was something new, something we'd never experienced before. Until Chippy upped and left we all thought we were the best going. The best in every way. But not now. Even the girls stopped following the team once Chippy left. When that happened we knew for certain there *was* something wrong with us. We felt that bad we were on the verge of ringing the Samaritans. But we gave up on that because every time we rang the phone was engaged.

The only good thing about it was I got back

into writing again. I wrote a poison letter to High-Lowe over poaching Chippy. I had the letter photo-copied thirty-two times, and addressed them in different handwriting, using different-sized envelopes. I posted them without any stamps; that way High-Lowe had to pay the postage. Mad Victor even sent him some worms he dug out of the garden.

A week later Harry Hennessy showed up at training with the *Evening Herald*.

'Look at this,' he said.

'What?'

'That there.'

There was a heading: 'Bees' Knees player, the new Liam Brady.'

'What's it about, Harry?'

'Read it.'

'Naw, we wanna know nothin' about Bees' Knees. You read it to us.'

'In John O'Brien, Bees' Knees United, that famous nursery of schoolboy talent, have produced yet another outstanding talent who is destined to play in the upper echelon of

English professional football. "Chippy" O'Brien is already being regarded as the best talent to come out of Ireland since Liam Brady … Every accolade should be given to this club for its remarkable coaching system which produces a player of such talent …'

'How could they write that? He's only with them a week. He's not really their player. He was always ours.'

Mr Glynn didn't bother answering, he was too much in the dumps. Instead, Harry Hennessy did the talking.

'It's like that with most of the big schoolboy clubs. They get the credit for everythin'. Clubs like us only get the blame. That's the way it is, an' always will be.'

Maybe what Harry said was true. Anyway, it made us seethe all the more. We couldn't wait to get at Bees' Knees United. We were due to play them at home in the People's Park in a few weeks' time.

'Don't worry, Mr Glynn, we'll clobber 'm. Nobody beats us in the Park. Not that crowd, anyway.'

# 14  A Return Match

Every one of us trained extra hard for the match. We even gave up the fags. Mr Glynn brought us back to his house and made us eat porridge and plenty of chicken soup. We didn't complain, especially Victor. He was up to everything on offer. He began to look that healthy you could see the colour come back into his cheeks.

By the time the match came around we were rearing to go. The same couldn't be said of Chippy. He hardly tried. You could see his heart wasn't in it. The Bees' Knees management went spare. They didn't like watching Chippy going through the motions without putting in any great effort. High-Lowe had a real go at Chippy, shouting and roaring and giving out like mad. But it wasn't entirely Chippy's fault, he just hadn't got the heart to outdo his mates, that's all. Even though he had left the team he was still one of us.

But High-Lowe didn't see things that way.

'Get stuck in, O'Brien!' that's all he could say. 'Make an effort, you lazy sod!'

It wasn't nice for Chippy out on the pitch. We could all sense that, and the more High-Lowe shouted abuse at Chippy, the more we felt for him. That didn't stop us from getting stuck into the other players though. We gave them hell.

We were a goal up after ten minutes. Growler Hughes came forward for a corner and scored with a downward header. The goal-keeper hadn't an earthly. We ran straight to Growler, hugged the living daylights out of him, before going back to the centre-circle for the ball to be recentred. Some of us even had time to give High-Lowe the two-fingers. We weren't that stupid to do it in front of the referee. We did it behind his back.

Growler's goal inspired us. We strung passes together all over the place. What's more we moved like greased lightning. You'd think we'd never seen a fag in our lives, we were that fit. We got to the ball first every time.

Eight minutes later we scored a second goal. Sean Holden played the ball through the middle. Flintstone, above all people, latched on to it and slotted it wide of the goal-keeper into the back of the net.

We hadn't time to hug him though. Soon as he scored the goal he sprinted off on a lap of the pitch, his hands held high. You'd think the Park was full of spectators, but it wasn't. There was only Mr Glynn, Harry Hennessy, a few subs, High-Lowe and his coaching staff, not to mention the trees on the roadside of the Park. The way Flintstone took off you'd think he'd just scored the winning goal in front of the Liverpool faithful at Anfield.

We were three up by half-time. Growler again. He barged into the penalty area and flattened their centre-half before planting the ball into the net.

The referee allowed the goal to stand. High-Lowe went spare. He tore Chippy out of it at half-time. Took him off ten minutes into the second half, and almost had a seizure when we rammed in two more goals and went on to

115

win 5-0. It was slaughter.

Slaughter!

Our biggest win of the season.

When the match was over, High-Lowe raved on about us being a crowd of wasters, nothing better than delinquents.

'When my players will be playin' at the top level, you lot will be nothin'! You haven't the character, dedication, the stayin' power. You lot are nothin'!'

Chippy heard it all. There was High-Lowe trying to make out that his lot were superior to us, not just as footballers, but as people. That in years to come, when his players would be at the top, we'd have ended up alcoholics like Mad Victor's uncles, or worse, locked up in jail.

Jail?

Yeah, he said that. Said we were only fit to be jail-birds.

We didn't like it one bit. Harry Hennessy would have clocked him, only he didn't feel too good. His blood-pressure was at him.

Soon as Chippy heard the insults he wanted nothing more to do with Bees' Knees United.

What's more, he told High-Lowe straight out.

'I'm not playin' for you any more,' he said.

'Is that so?'

'Yeah. I'm goin' back to me mates.'

'You won't be able to do that.'

'Why not?'

'The transfer dead-line was a few weeks ago.'

You could almost sense the despair in Chippy's face. He had had enough of High-Lowe. Even getting on the Irish Schoolboys team didn't seem as important as before. What he really wanted was to come back and play for us. But now he wouldn't be able to because the transfer dead-line was gone.

But Mr Glynn and Harry Hennessy soon sorted out that problem. They tore High-Lowe out of it. We all got in on the act.

'The lad's still our player. He doesn't need a transfer.'

'What d'ye mean, he doesn't need a transfer?'

'That form you got him on is botched. You got his name wrong. It's not even his signature. You're playing a protest there.'

'I don't play bangers.'

'Well, you are now. An' we won't be long in tellin' the other teams so.'

And we wouldn't. We'd tell everybody. There'd be protests and rows all over the place. Say what they like, Chippy was still a Riverside player. He wouldn't be going anywhere. He'd be staying put with us.

What's more, we'd be in touch with the newspapers to let them know Chippy always belonged to us, not High-Lowe. That would really get to Bees' Knees. It would make them as sick as parrots.

We left the Park as happy as Larry. And why wouldn't we?

We had not only beaten Bees' Knees United, we'd also got our star player back.

We knew how High-Lowe felt.

Humiliated.

That made us glad – real glad.

## 15  Another Big Surprise

Mad Victor got a letter in the post. The letter was from some woman who said she was his mother. She was coming home to live in Bray and had bought a new house. She was bringing a new daddy with her, plus a half-sister for Victor and Henry. Their new sister was named Cleo. She was four and a half. Victor and Henry could baby-sit her, bring her out to play on the swings, take her for a paddle down the sea front. They'd all be living in the new house, Victor and Henry included.

The new daddy was as rich as sin. The eyes nearly popped out of Victor's head with delight when he read that part of the letter. He even had a fancy car with an English registration.

Mad Victor figured this new daddy would suit him fine, especially if he were as rich as the letter stated. His old daddy, whoever or wherever he was, could go to hell. He told us all about the letter.

'I've got a new daddy. He smokes cigars. Big ones from Cuba.'

'That makes him a Yank.'

'No, he's Jamaican.'

'Jamaican? That makes him black as soot.'

'So wha'? I've a little sister, too.'

'That so?'

'Yeah. I'm going to call her Princess, an' brin' her to all our matches.'

'You will not!'

'I will.'

Mad Victor and Henry were real keen to meet their mother and new family. They had to wait three weeks, but it wasn't long in passing. Most of us were just as interested. We even went to inspect the new house where Victor and Henry were going to live. There was a driveway, and a lawn the size of two football pitches. The house was three storeys high. It was so big you could race greyhounds around the corridors. We were impressed. Victor's new da had to be a millionaire, the richest man in all of Jamaica.

As things turned out Victor's new da *was* black. But his name was Terry O'Sullivan: an *Irish* name. We couldn't understand how he had an Irish name. It completely mystified us. It still does. It takes some beating how a real-life Jamaican could have an Irish name.

Victor's little sister is a real dote. Soon as Victor brought her to our matches we took a shine to her. We wouldn't call her anything but Princess, because that's what she is – a princess. If anyone as much as calls her names we're in straight away, every one of us. We wouldn't have anyone upset her. Even Harry Hennessy feels that way. He doesn't curse when she's around. In fact, none of us do, that's how much we think of her.

It came as a real surprise to Victor and Henry to find themselves living in luxury. It surprised Mrs O'Leary too. And our head teacher. Where before Victor was barred, now he was allowed into school, though he was a class below us. He didn't mind in the least. All he wanted was to be accepted. He was well accepted now, thanks to 'Pop Terry's' millions.

Thinking back on Mad Victor ending up with a rich da just shows how life is full of surprises.

I even had a surprise of my own lately. There's a film studios here in Bray, Ardmore Studios. One day a man came to our house and asked to see my da.

'There's this man at the door wants to see you, Da.'

'Tell him to go away.'

'He says it might be worth a few bob to you.'

Straight away Da was up off the sofa and out to see what the man wanted.

'I believe you have a peculiar laugh.'

'Who told ye so?'

'Just someone.'

'Well, ye can tell "just someone" to go an' mind his own bloody business. There's nothin' wrong with the way I laugh. D'ye hear me? There's nothin' wrong!'

'There could be some money in it for you.'

'You sick, or wha'?'

'No. I'm involved in a film due to be shot in Ardmore soon. We need a certain laugh for a voice-over. I've been told your laugh might suit to a tee.'

'That so? Wha's the name of the film?'

'It's a remake of a film made years ago.'

'Wha' film?'

'*Francis the Talking Mule!*'

'Go to hell!'

My da went ape, cursed the man all the way to the front gate, and told him not to come back.

Me, Ma and my sisters didn't think the

same way, though. We thought it a waste. Da could have been a film star and we'd have plenty of money. It was an opportunity lost – the chance of a lifetime down the drain.

Still there's plenty to look forward to. There's our trip to London in April. There's the chance of Chippy getting on the Irish Schoolboys team.

Like my granda said, thirty seconds before he died, 'Where there's life there's hope – Bob Hope.'

Maybe my biro will strike paper and I'll write a best-seller.

Maybe …

See you in April.

Maybe …

*Peter Regan*
## Riverside: The Street League

Mrs O'Leary has a GREAT IDEA. Start a street-league! To keep all the tea-leaves around the place out of trouble. And get a little publicity – which might come in handy in view of impending Council elections.
Riverside to a man – or a U-14 – rise to the challenge. Which team will bring home the Brenda O'Leary Perpetual Cup?
But, of course, football is not the only thing on their minds. Chippy has his gran to worry about. Jimmy has to sort out his da, write a book, and dream about the beautiful Heather McFadden. Mad Victor has his own ideas; especially where Mrs O'Leary is concerned …

*Illustrated by Terry Myler • 112 pages • £2.95*

*Peter Regan*
# Riverside: The Croke Park Conspiracy

It's the witching hour of night and two shadowy
figures are stealing across the People's Park.
One of them produces a bushman saw and
they start sawing. A few minutes later, the skinny
GAA goal-posts are in the river.
Naturally there's blue murder and Mrs O'Leary
(now Councillor O'Leary) springs into action.
Handbag at the ready.
Riverside Boys v the GAA is on!
In between skirmishes, Chippy has a great idea,
Brains O'Mahony has another, and Mad Victor
and Mad Henry see a bit of the world.
Jimmy has something else on his mind – who, in
the absence of his masterpiece, *Forlorn Love,* will
win the Book-of-the-Year Award!

*Illustrated by Terry Myler • 112 pages • £2.95*

PETER REGAN, born in north Roscommon, now lives in Bray, where he runs a small fuel and seed business. He once managed a schoolboy team, and as 'Chick' Regan masterminded the Avon Glens and Brighton Celtic.

He has written three soccer books: *Urban Heroes*, *Teen Glory* and *Young Champions*, which have been very successful here and have also been translated into several European languages. He has also written two fantasy books: *Touchstone* and *Revenge of the Wizards*.

*Riverside v City Slickers* is the third in the 'Riverside' series; the other two are *Riverside: The Street League* and *Riverside: The Croke Park Conspiracy*. A fourth is on the way.